Pete the Cat
My First I Can Draw

Harperfestival is an imprint of HarperCollins Publishers.

Pete the Cat: My First I Can Draw
Copyright © 2016 by James Dean
All rights reserved. Manufactured in China.
No part of this book may be used or reproduced in any manner whatsoever
without written permission except in the case of brief quotations embodied in
critical articles and reviews. For information address HarperCollins Children's Books,
a division of HarperCollins Publishers, 195 Broadway, New York, NY 10007.
www.harpercollinschildrens.com

Library of Congress Control Number: 2016932100
ISBN 978-0-06-230443-8
Design by Lori S Malkin
16 17 18 19 20 SCP 10 9 8 7 6 5 4 3 2 1
❖
First Edition

Pete the Cat

My First

I Can Draw

by James Dean

HARPER FESTIVAL
An Imprint of HarperCollinsPublishers

In this book you will use a lot of different shapes
to draw Pete and his world.

Here are some basic shapes you will use. Try a few out
here first and then you'll be ready to go!

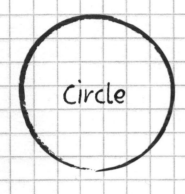

Circle

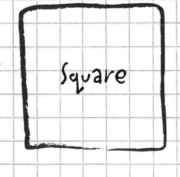

Square

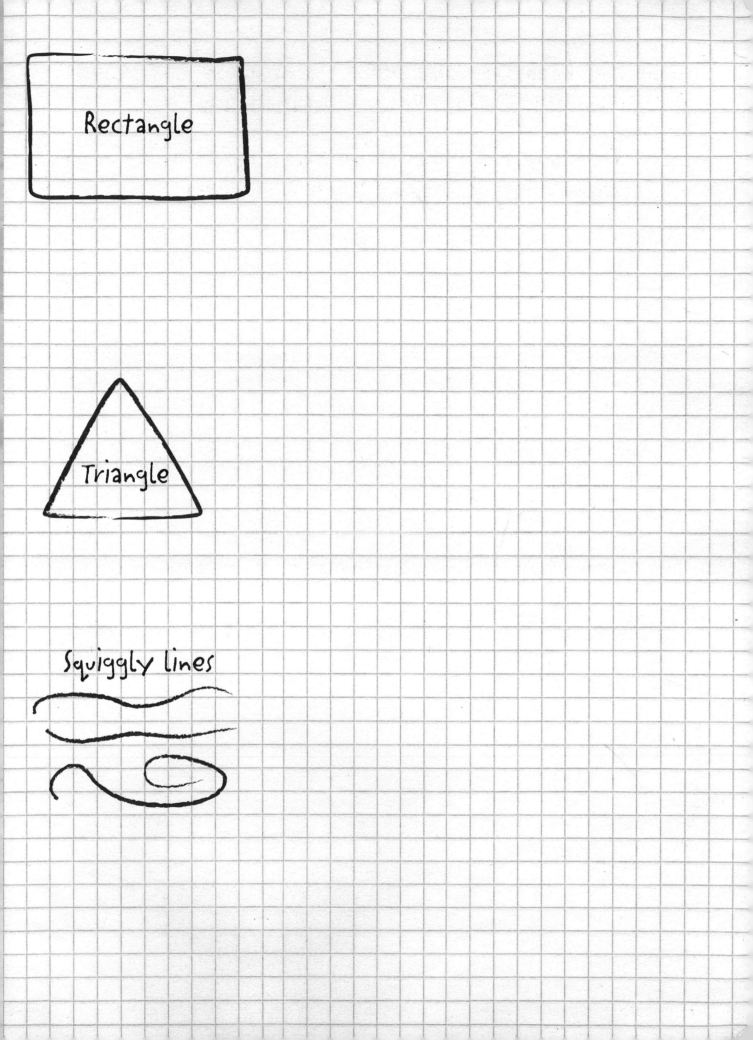

Meet Pete

Draw him.

1.   2.   3.   4.

Now try drawing Pete on your own!

US MAIL 1215

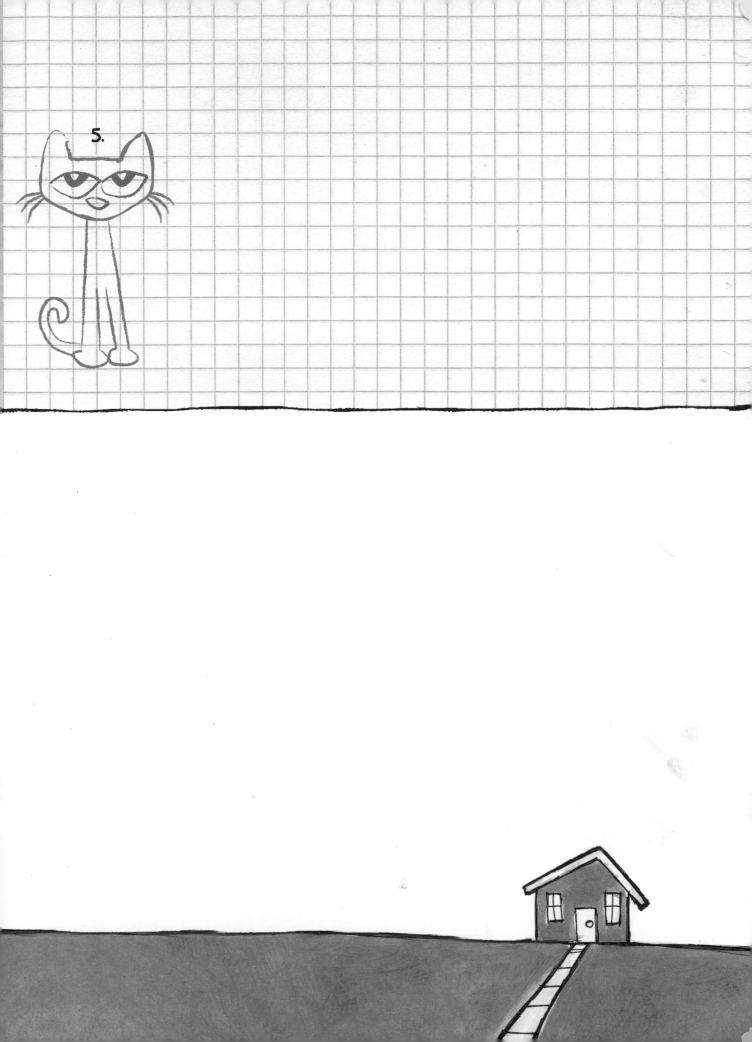

5.

Pete's New Shoes

Draw Pete with his new shoes.

Now try drawing Pete on your own!
Decorate his new shoes.

Pete on the Move

Draw Pete taking
a walk.

1.

2.

3.

4.

Now try drawing Pete walking on your own!

Pete on a Roll

1.

2.

3.

4.

Now try drawing Pete skateboarding on your own!

CATALINA PKWY

Draw Pete riding
his skateboard.

Rock On, Pete

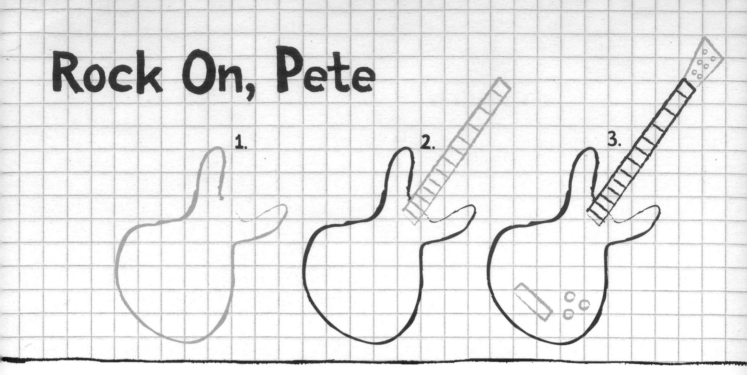

1.
2.
3.

Now try drawing Pete playing his guitar!

MUSIC LESSONS

Draw Pete's
new guitar.

4.

Pete's Mom

1.

2.

3.

4.

5.

6.

Try drawing
Pete's mom.

Now try drawing Pete and his mom!

Pete's Dad

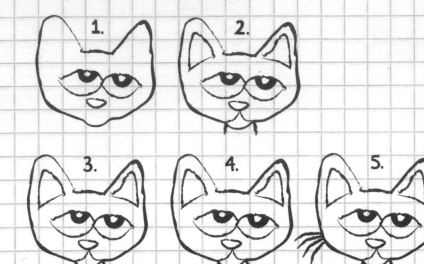

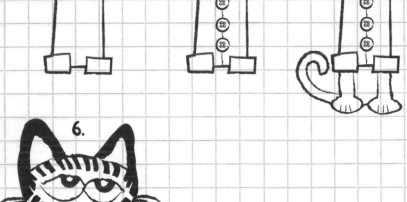

Try drawing
Pete's dad.

Now try drawing Pete and his dad!

Brother Bob

Try drawing Pete's
brother, Bob.

Now try drawing Pete and
his whole family!

All Aboard

Draw Pete in
the caboose.

1.

2.

3.

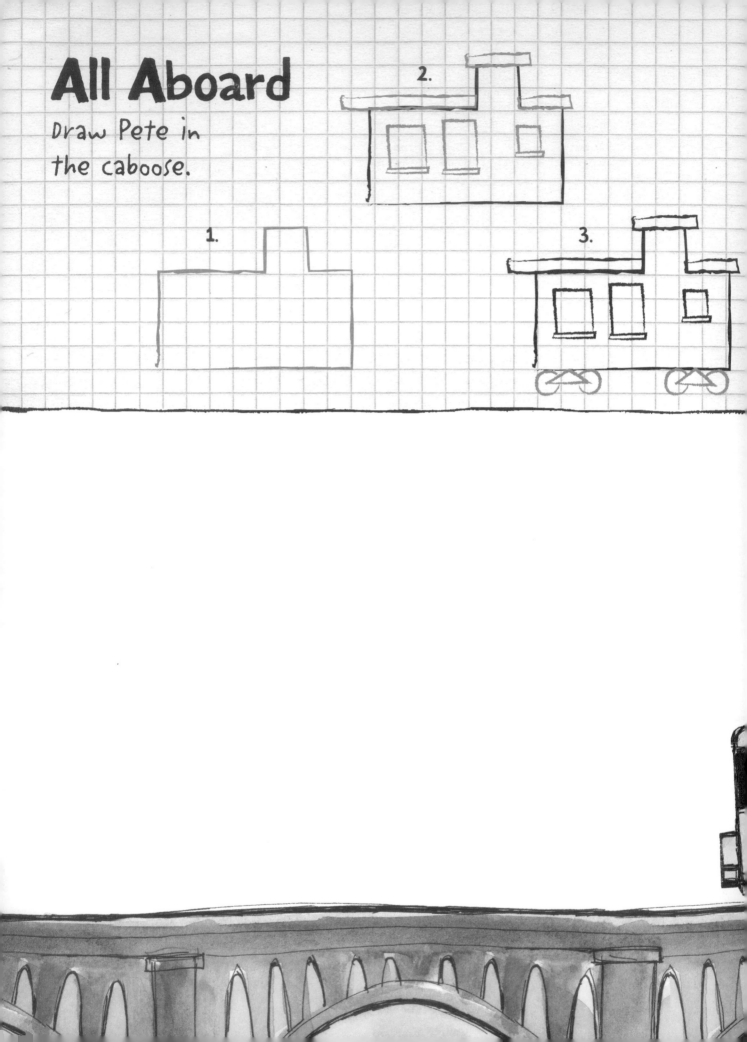

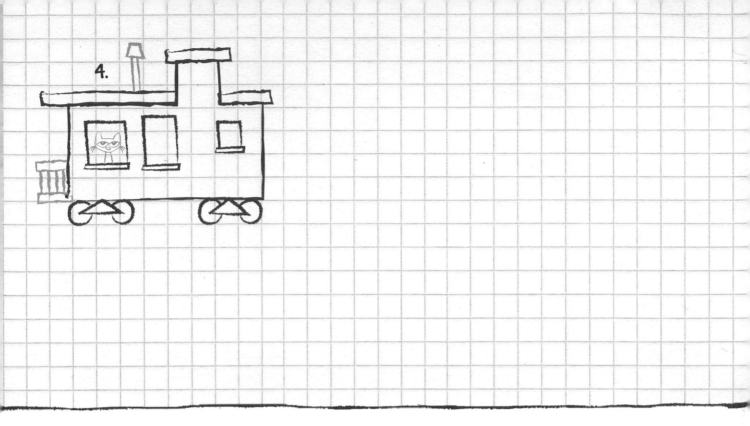

4.

Now add the caboose to the train!

Ticket to Ride

Draw the
train conductor.

1.

2.

3.

4.

5.

6.

7.

Now try drawing the train conductor collecting Pete's ticket.

Meet the Engineer

Draw the engineer.

1.

2.

3.

4.

5.

6.

7.

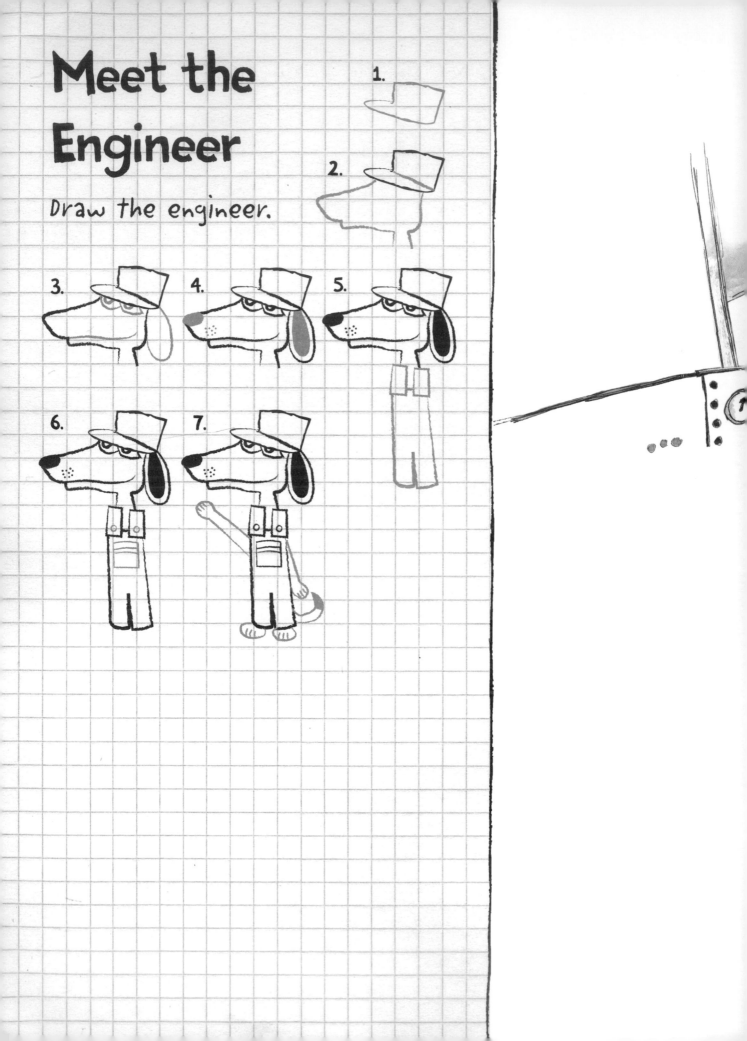

Now try drawing Pete and the engineer in the head car.

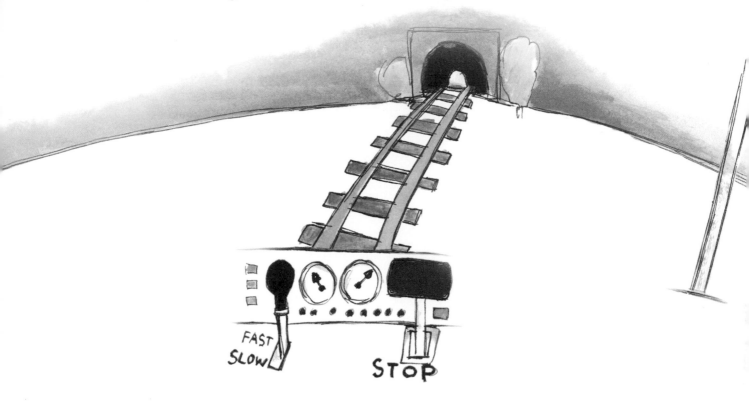

Behind the Wheel

Draw the train.

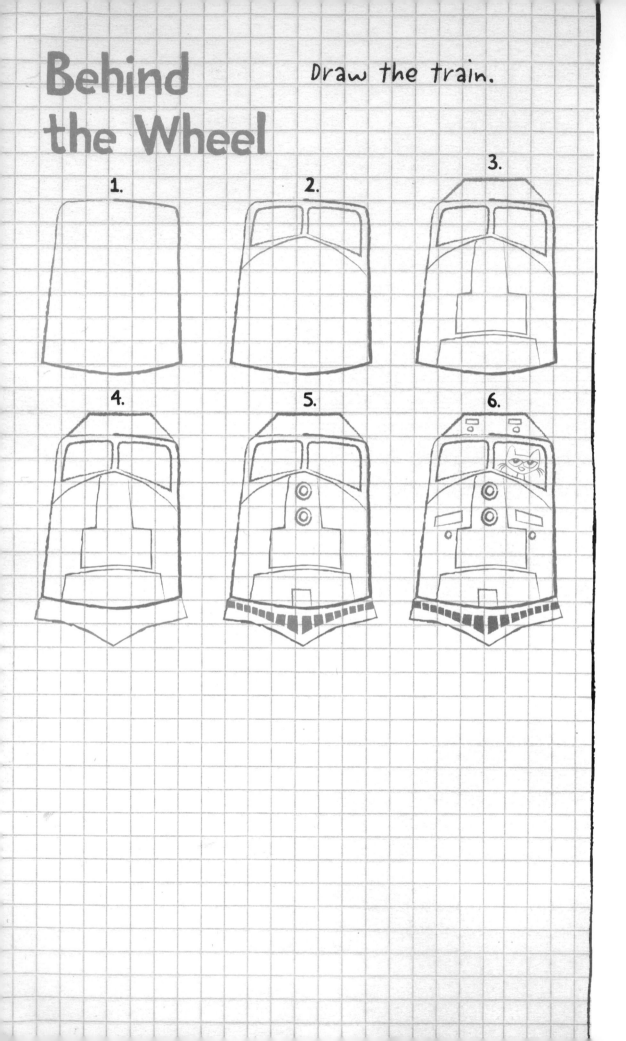

1.

2.

3.

4.

5.

6.

Now try drawing Pete driving the train on your own!

Pete's Grandma

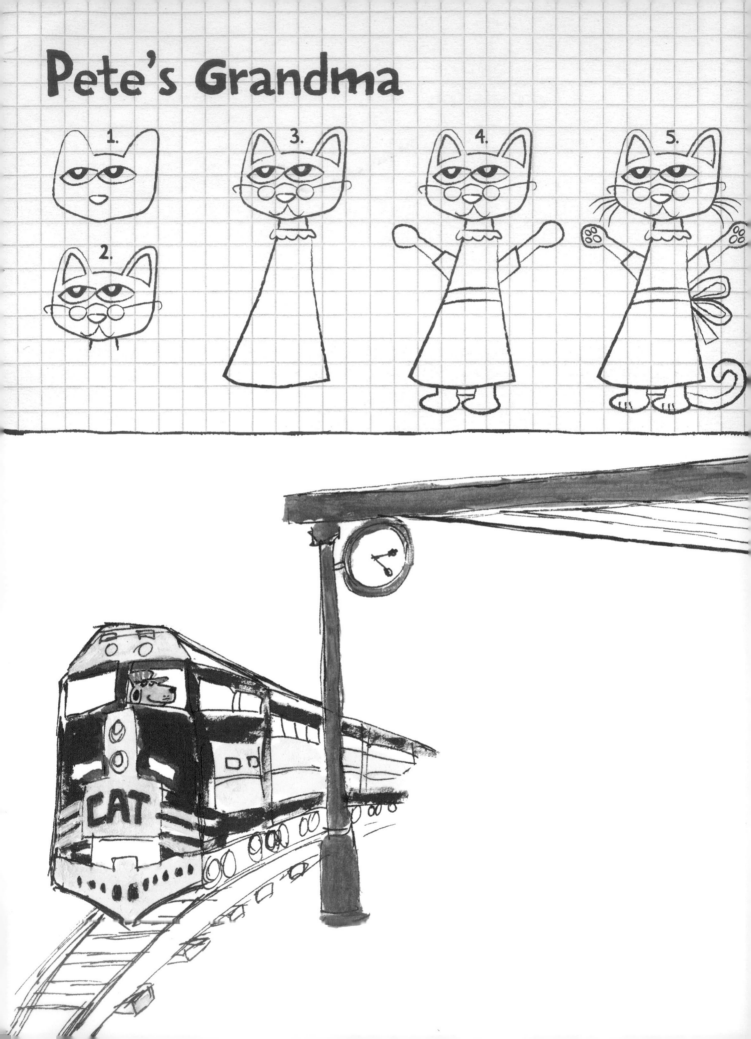

Draw Pete's grandma.

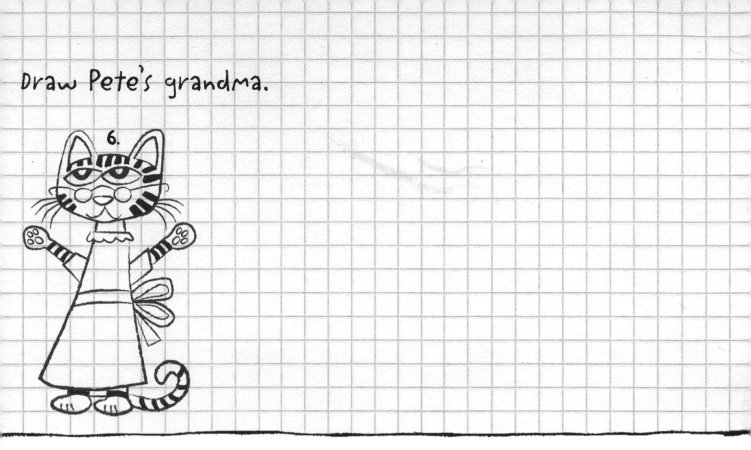

6.

Pete's grandma is waiting for him at the train station. Draw them!

Robo-Pete

Draw Pete's robot.

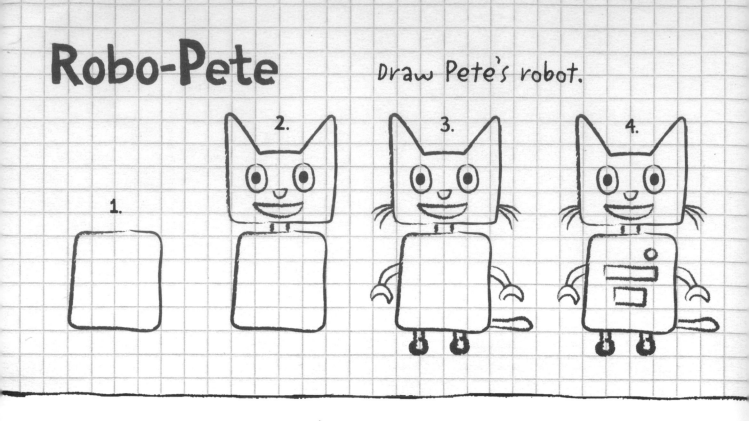

1.   2.   3.   4.

Now try drawing Pete's robot on your own!

Prehistoric Pete

Draw Cavecat Pete.

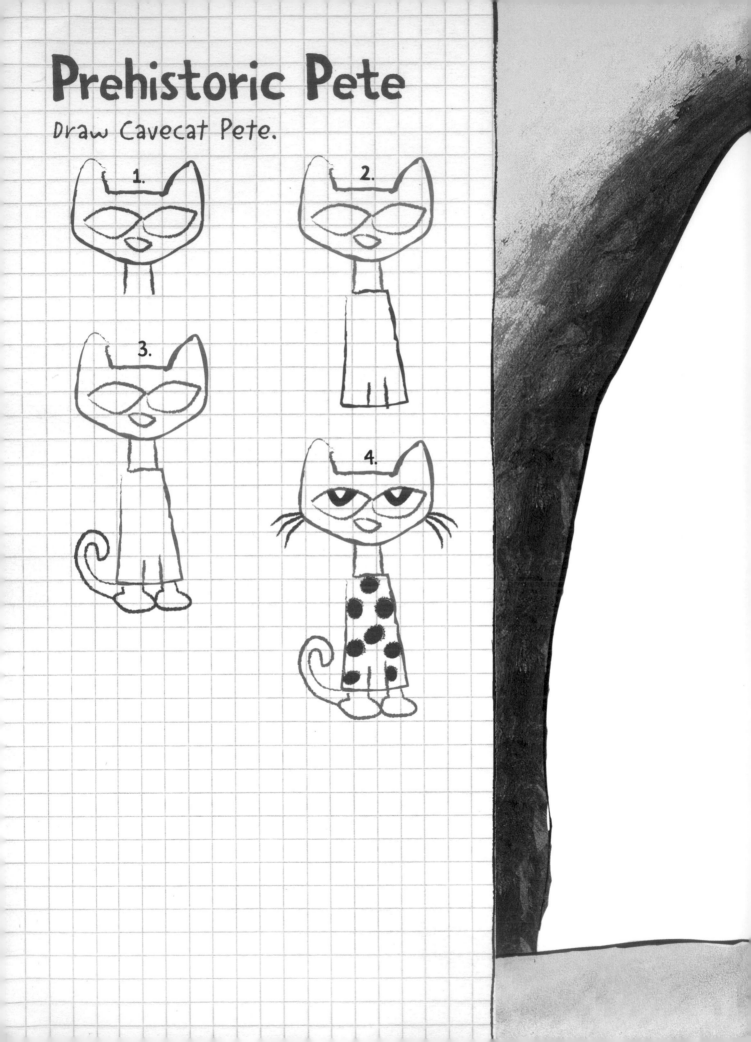

1.
2.
3.
4.

Try drawing
Cavecat Pete
on your own!

Terri the Pterosaur

Draw Terri
the Pterosaur.

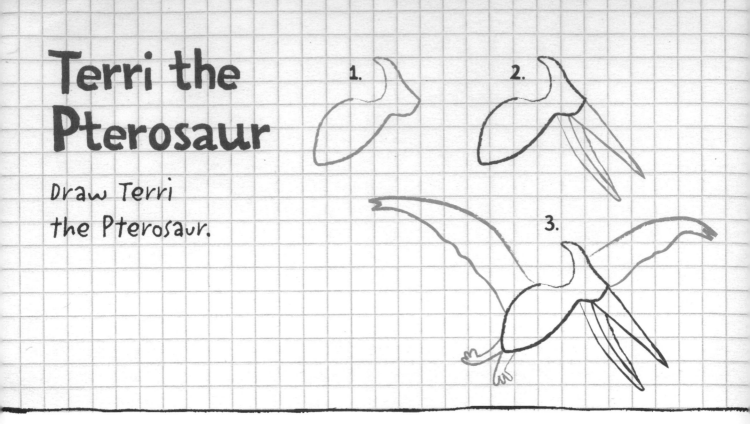

1.

2.

3.

Now try drawing Terri on your own!

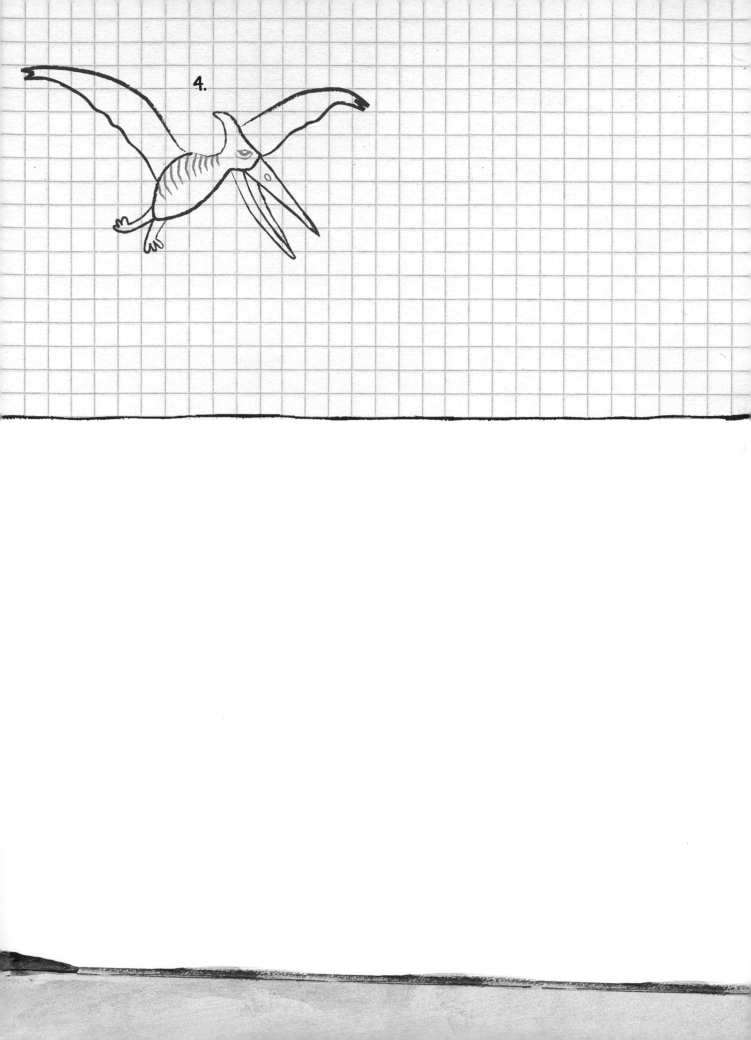

4.

High-Flying

Now try drawing Pete and Terri flying on your own!

Ethel the Apatosaurus

Draw Ethel
the Apatosaurus.

1.

2.

3.

4.

Now try drawing Ethel on your own!

Tall Trees

Draw the tall trees.

1. 2. 3.

Now try drawing Pete and Ethel in the trees on your own!

Way Up High

Draw Pete's telescope.

1.

2.

3.

4.

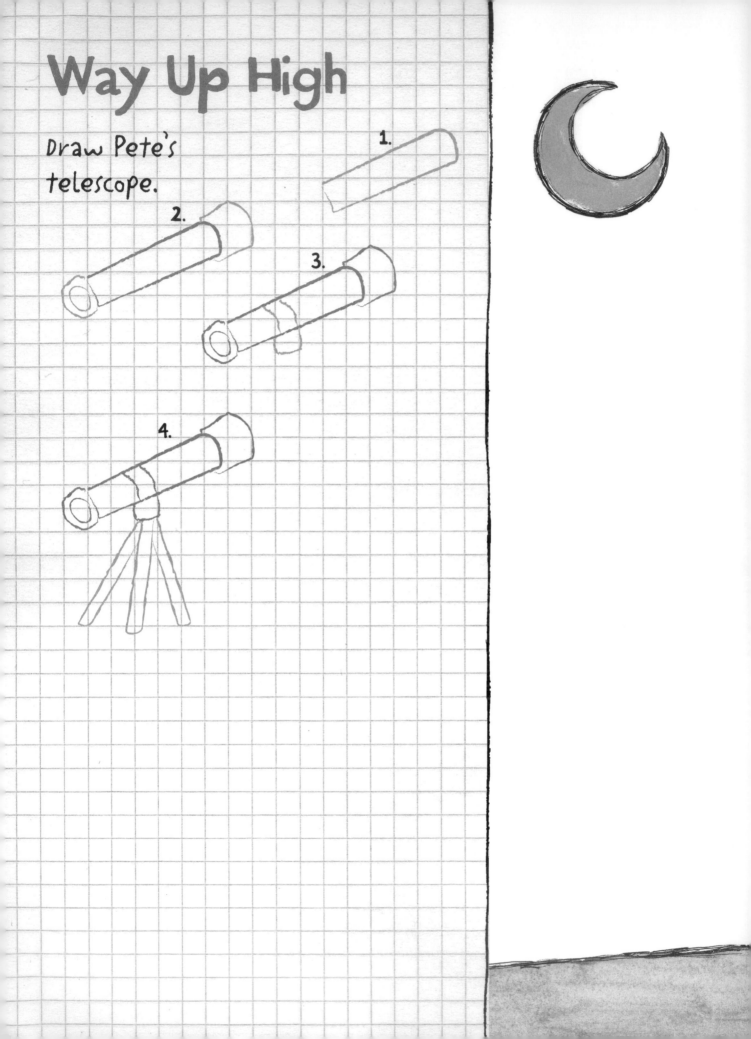

Now try drawing Pete and
his telescope on your own!

Bedtime Jams

Now try drawing Pete and his pj's on your own!

5.

Draw Pete's
starry pajamas.

Rocket Man

Draw Pete
flying a
rocket ship.

1.

2.

3.

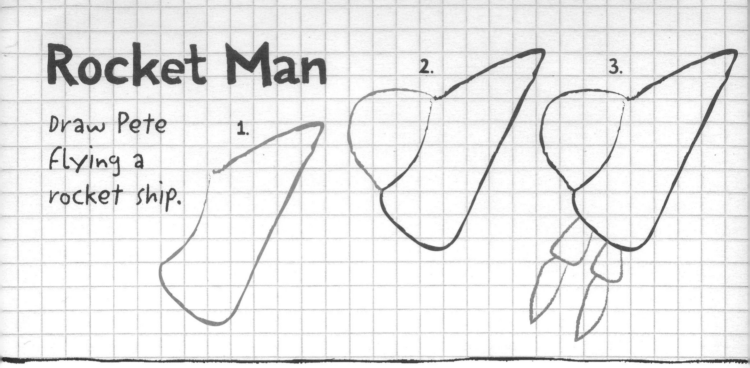

Now try drawing Pete's rocket ship on your own!

BED TIME
STORIES
for
CATS

THE CAT
and
the
FIDDLE

4.

Hanging Out
with Marty

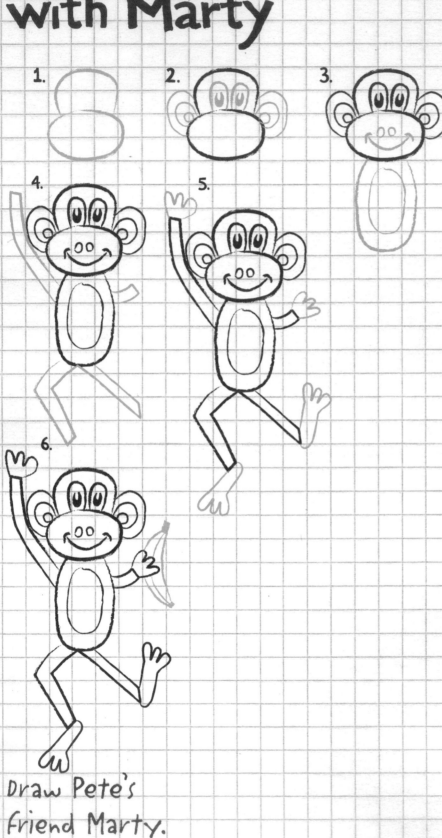

1.

2.

3.

4.

5.

6.

Draw Pete's
friend Marty.

Now try drawing Pete and Marty hanging out on your own!

Grumpy Toad

Draw Pete's friend
Grumpy Toad.

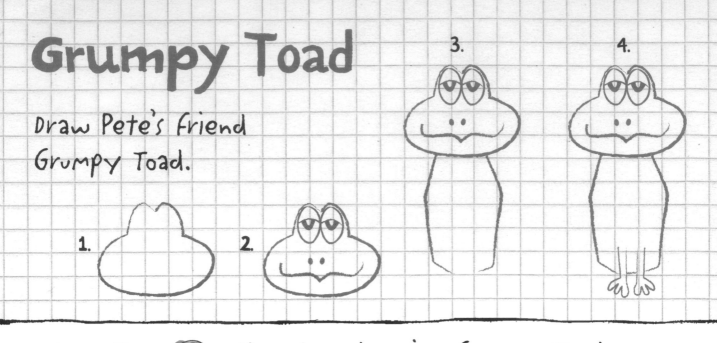

1.

2.

Now try drawing Grumpy Toad on
your own!

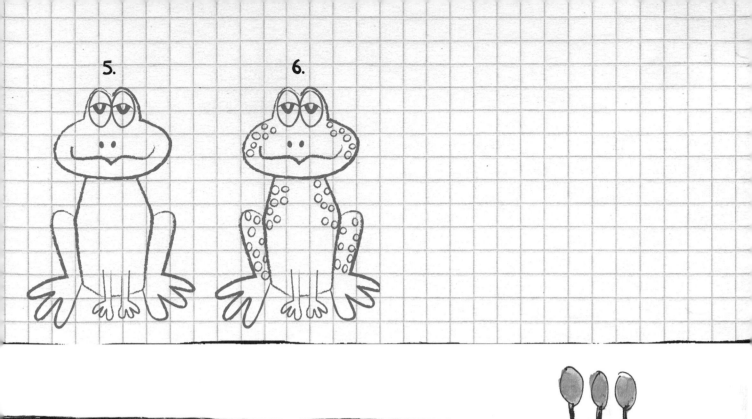

5.

6.

Emma

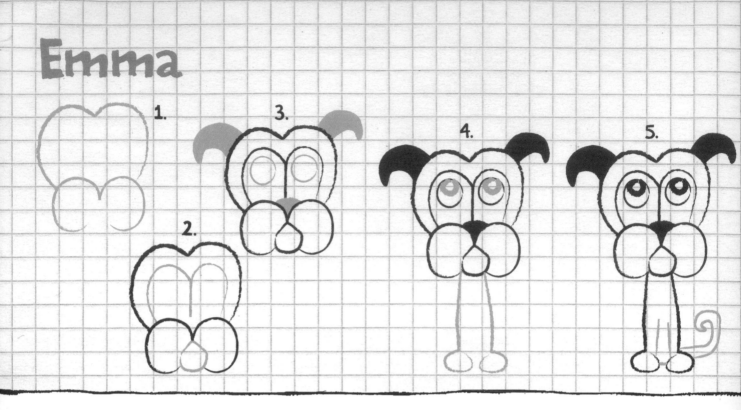

1.

2.

3.

4.

5.

Now try drawing Emma on your own!

Draw Pete's pal Emma.

6.

Callie

Draw Pete's friend Callie.

1.

2.

3.

4.

US MAIL 1215

Now try drawing Callie on your own!

Bus Stop Buddies

Draw Pete, Callie, and their lunch boxes.

Now try drawing the bus stop buddies on your own!

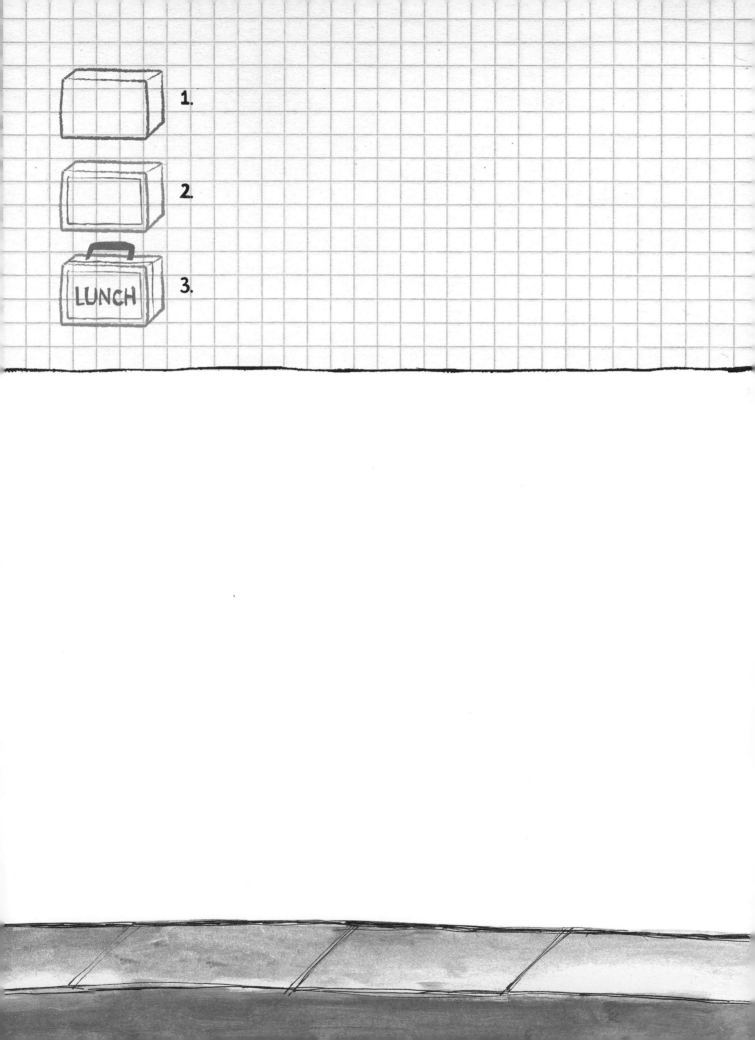

1.

2.

LUNCH   3.

The Wheels on the Bus

Draw the bus.

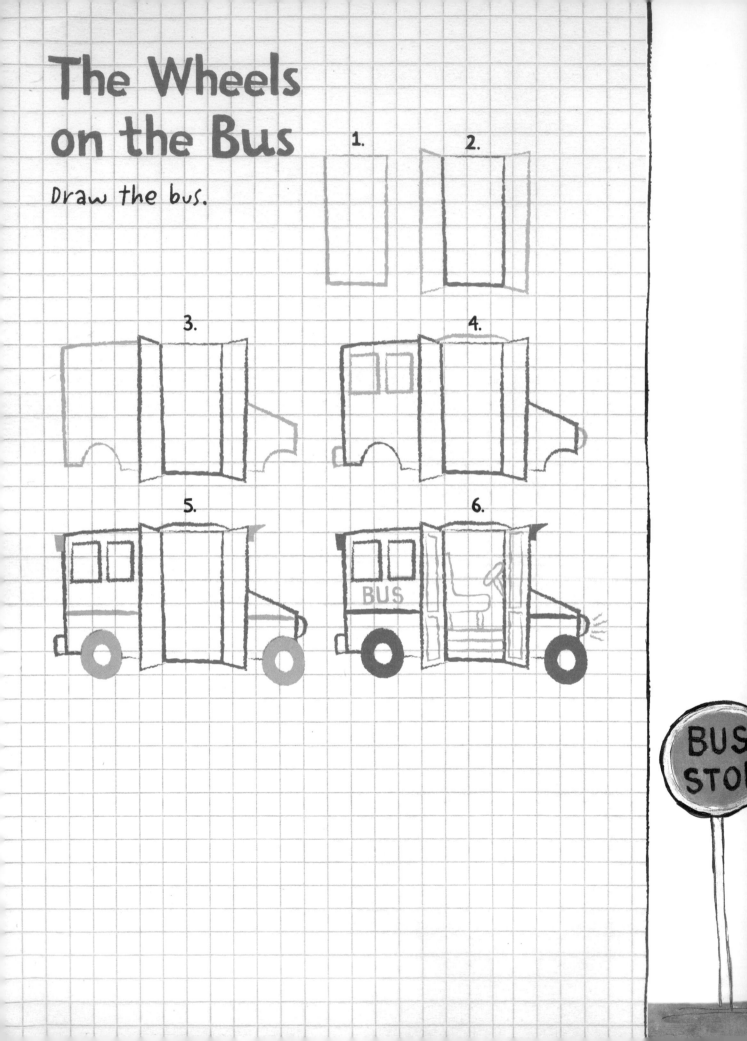

1.

2.

3.

4.

5.

6.

BUS

BUS
STO

Now try drawing Pete in the driver's seat on your own!

A Bouquet for Mom

Now try drawing Pete giving the flowers to his mom.

Draw the flowers Pete picked for his mom.

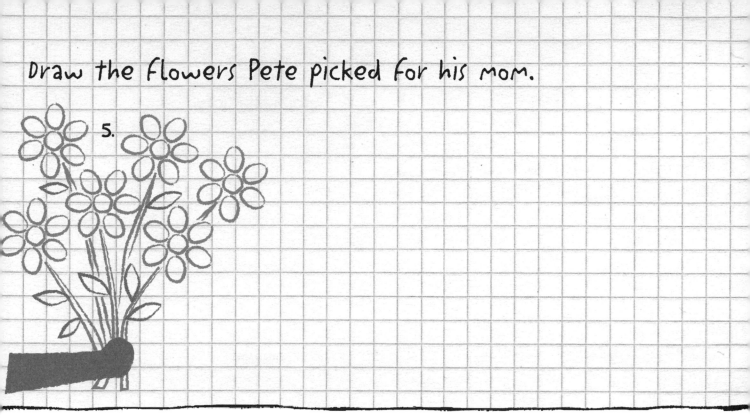

5.

Farmer Pete

1. 2. 3. 4.

Now try drawing Farmer Pete on your own!

Draw Farmer Pete.

5.

Pete's Pickup

Draw Pete driving
his pickup truck.

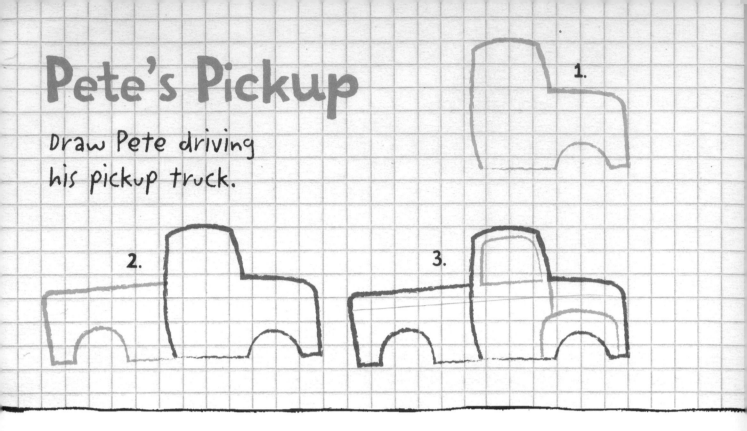

1.

2.

3.

Now try drawing Pete driving to the farm!

4.

5.

Cluck-Cluck

Draw the chicken.

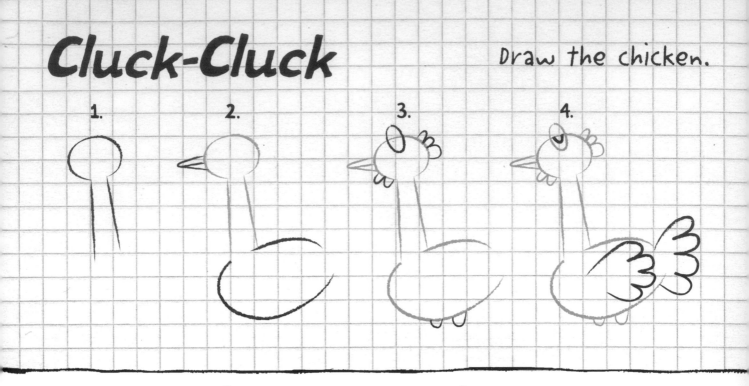

Now try drawing Pete and the chicken!

5.

Moo-Moo

Draw the cow.

1.

2.

3.

4.

5.

6.

Now try drawing Pete and the cow!

Oink-Oink
Draw the pig.

1.

2.

3.

4.

5.

Now try drawing Pete and the pig!

Baa-Baa

Now try drawing Pete and the goat!

Draw the goat.

5.

Quack-Quack

Draw the duck.

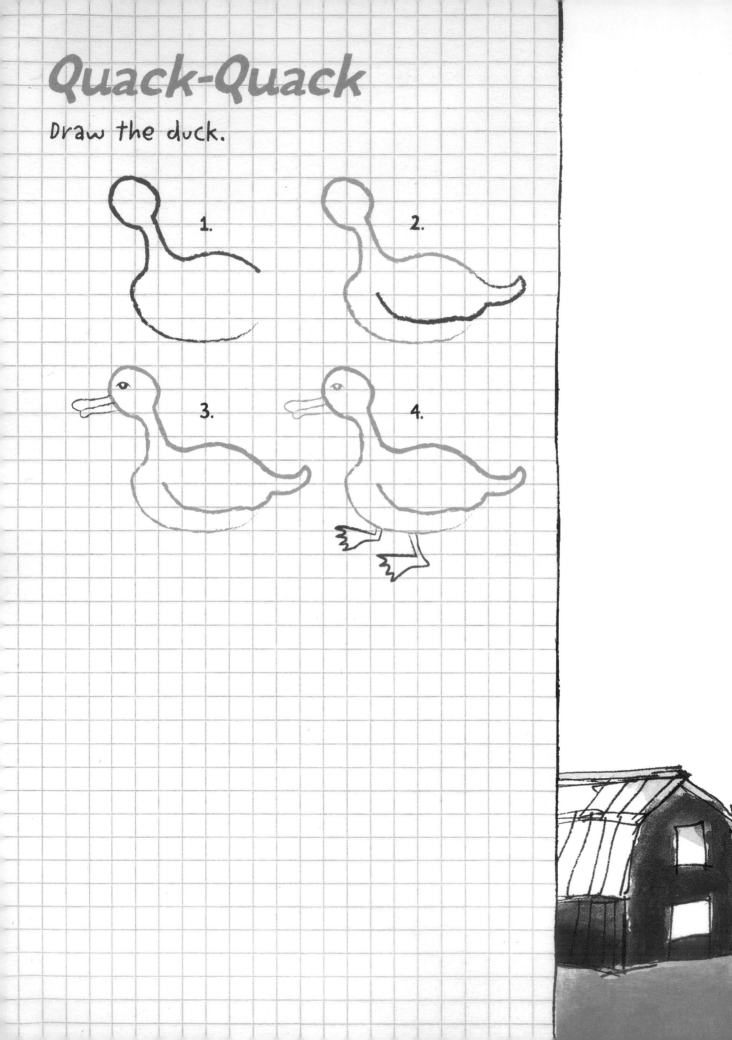

1.

2.

3.

4.

Now try drawing Pete and the duck!

Tractor Time

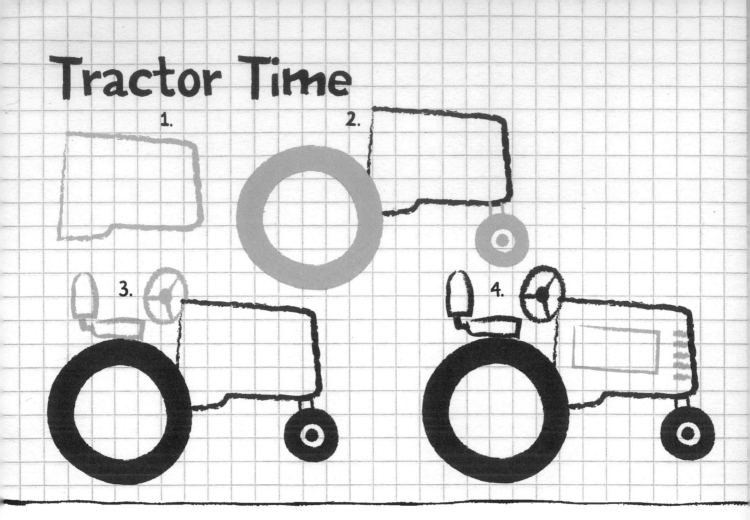

Now try drawing Pete driving the tractor!

Draw the tractor.

5.

Hee-Haw

Draw the donkey.

1.

2.

3.

4.

Now try drawing Pete riding on the donkey!

Maa-Maa

Draw the sheep.

1.

2.

3.

4.

5.

Now try drawing Pete and the sheep!

Pond Party

Pete plays his guitar for the barnyard animals. Draw them!

School Play

Draw the stage.

1.

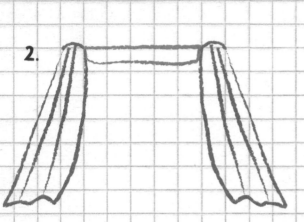

2.

3.

Now try drawing Pete and Callie performing on the stage!

Fun in the Sun

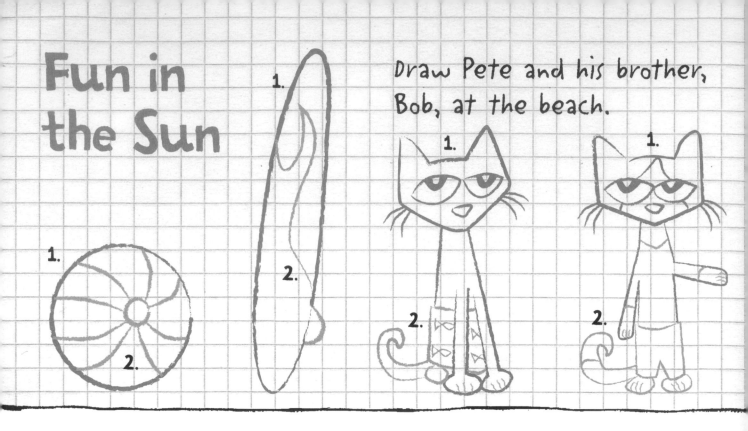

Draw Pete and his brother, Bob, at the beach.

Now try drawing Pete and Bob at the beach on your own!

King of
the Sand Castles

Draw the sand castle.

1.

2.

3.

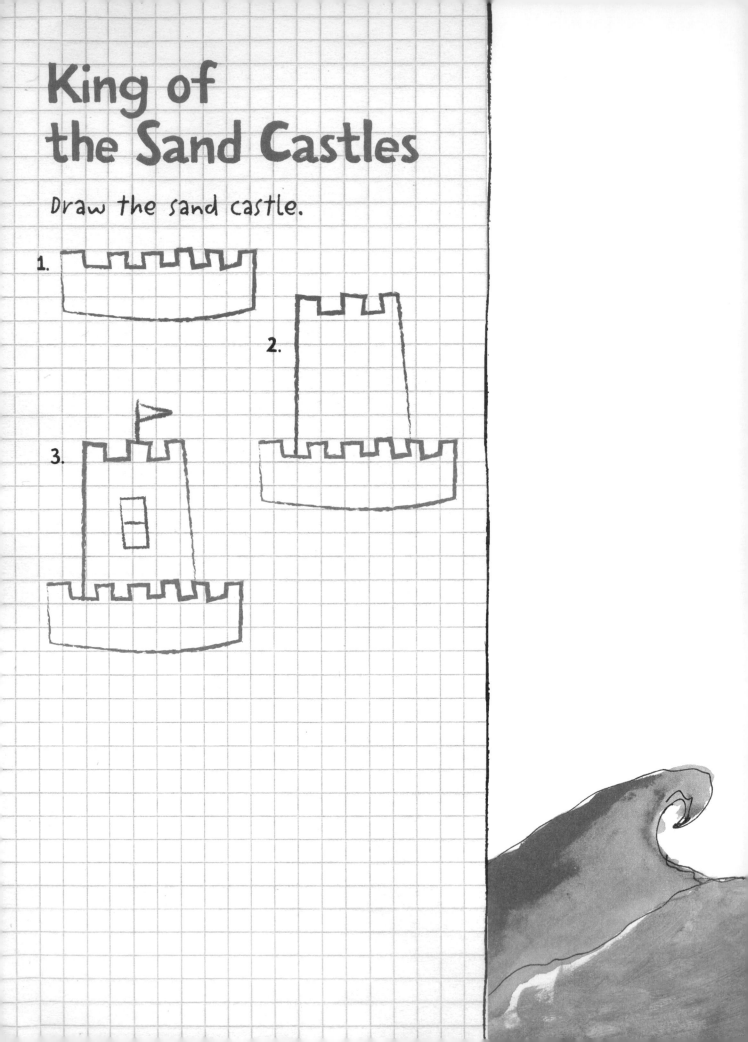

Now try drawing Pete with his sand castle!

Cowabunga Pete

Draw Pete and Bob riding a surfboard.

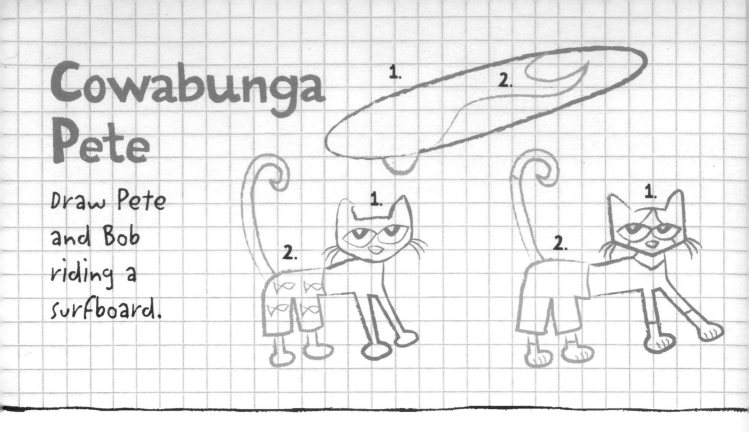

1.
2.

1.
2.

1.
2.

Now try drawing Pete and Bob riding the board together!

Grumpy on Guitar

Draw Grumpy Toad playing the guitar.

1.

2.

3.

4.

5.

Now try drawing Grumpy Toad strumming his guitar on your own!

Shake It, Squirrel

1.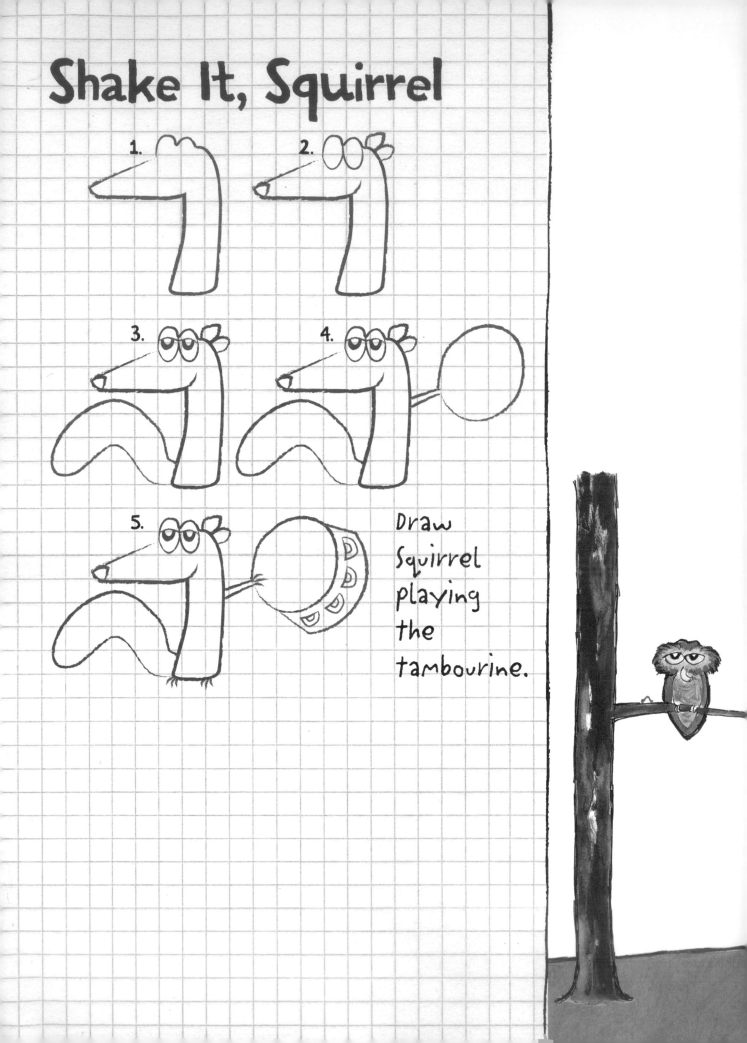

2.

3.

4.

5.

Draw Squirrel playing the tambourine.

Now try drawing Squirrel playing the tambourine on your own!

Blow, Alligator, Blow

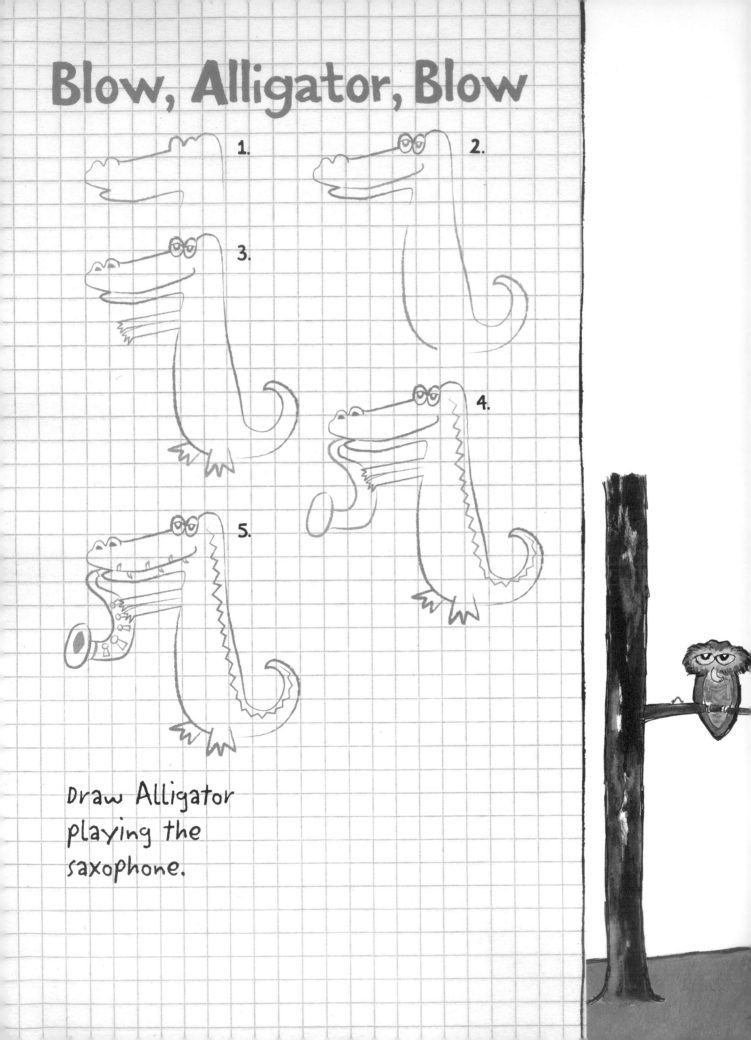

1.

2.

3.

4.

5.

Draw Alligator
playing the
saxophone.

Now try drawing Alligator playing the saxophone on your own!

Octopus Makes Music

Draw Octopus playing the keyboard.

1.

2.

3.

Now try drawing Octopus playing the keyboard on your own!

4.

5.

Gus Keeps the Beat

Draw Gus the Platypus playing the drums.

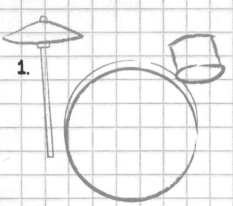

1.

2.

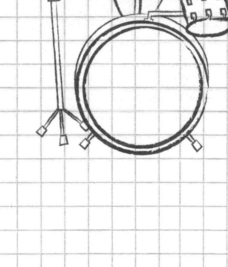

3.

4.

5.

Now try drawing Gus playing the drums on your own!

Band Jam

Now try drawing Pete and his band playing together!

Play Ball!

1. 2. 3. 4.

Now try drawing Pete on your own!

Draw Pete in his baseball uniform.

5.

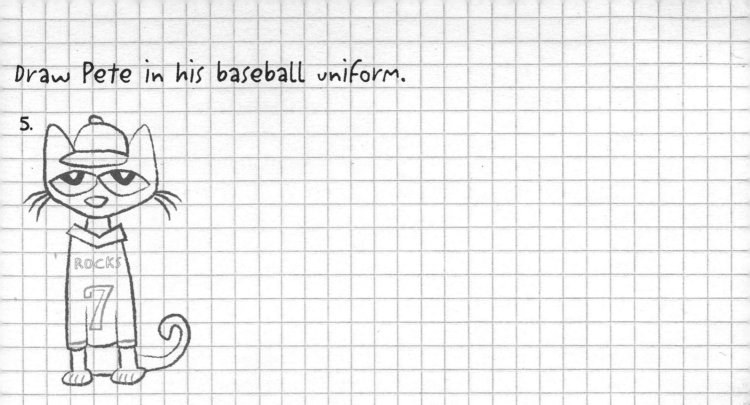

Batter Up!

Draw Pete up at bat.

1.

2.

3.

4.

5.

6.

ROCKS 7

Now try drawing Pete at bat on your own!

Outstanding in His Field

Draw Pete catching a fly ball.

1.

2.

3.

ROCKS
7

4.

ROCKS
7

Now try drawing Pete catching a fly ball on your own!

Build It, Pete

Draw Pete in his construction outfit.

1.

2.

3.

4.

5.

6.

Now try drawing Pete with his tool belt on your own!

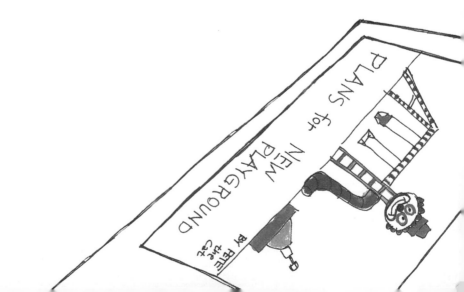

Turtle and the Wrecking Ball Crane

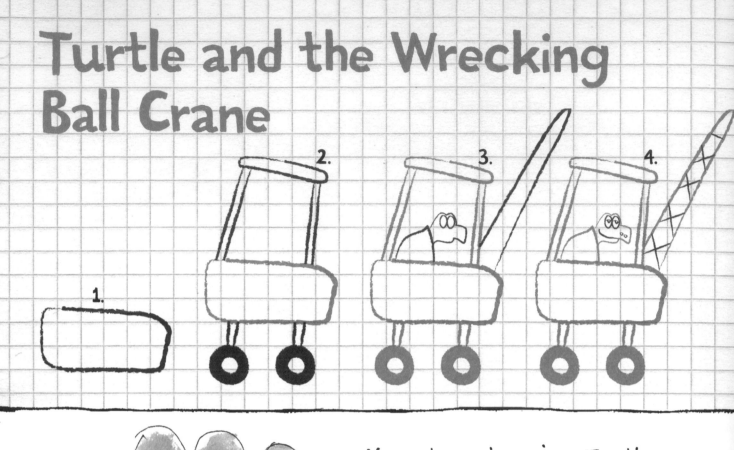

1.

2.

3.

4.

Now try drawing Turtle using the crane on your own!

Draw Turtle using the wrecking ball.

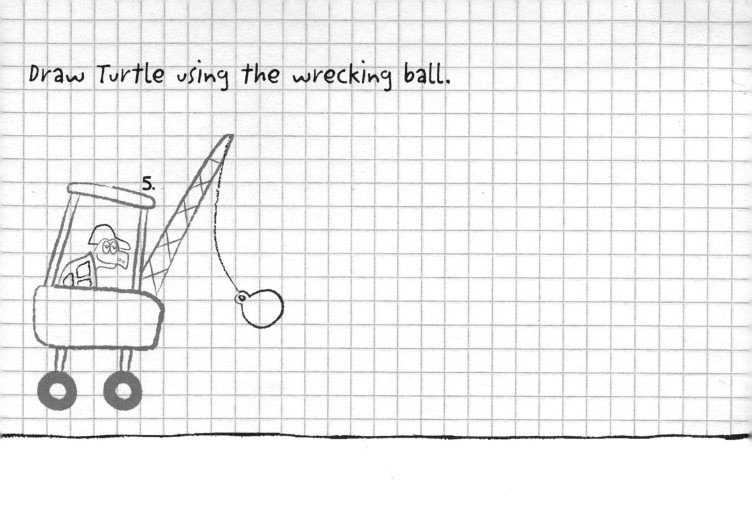

Toad and the Bulldozer

Draw Toad using the bulldozer.

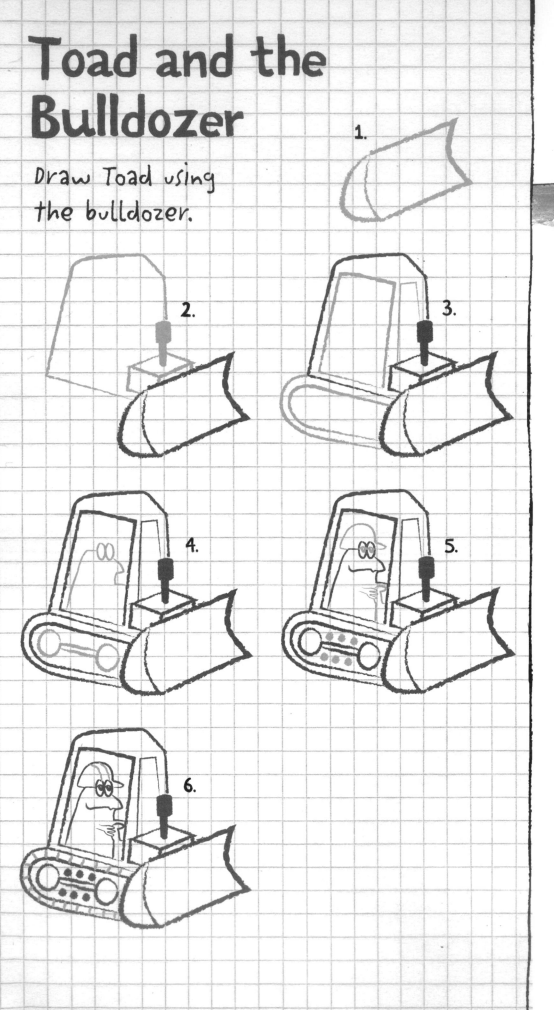

1.

2.

3.

4.

5.

6.

Now try drawing Toad using the bulldozer on your own!

Cow and the Backhoe

Draw Cow using the backhoe.

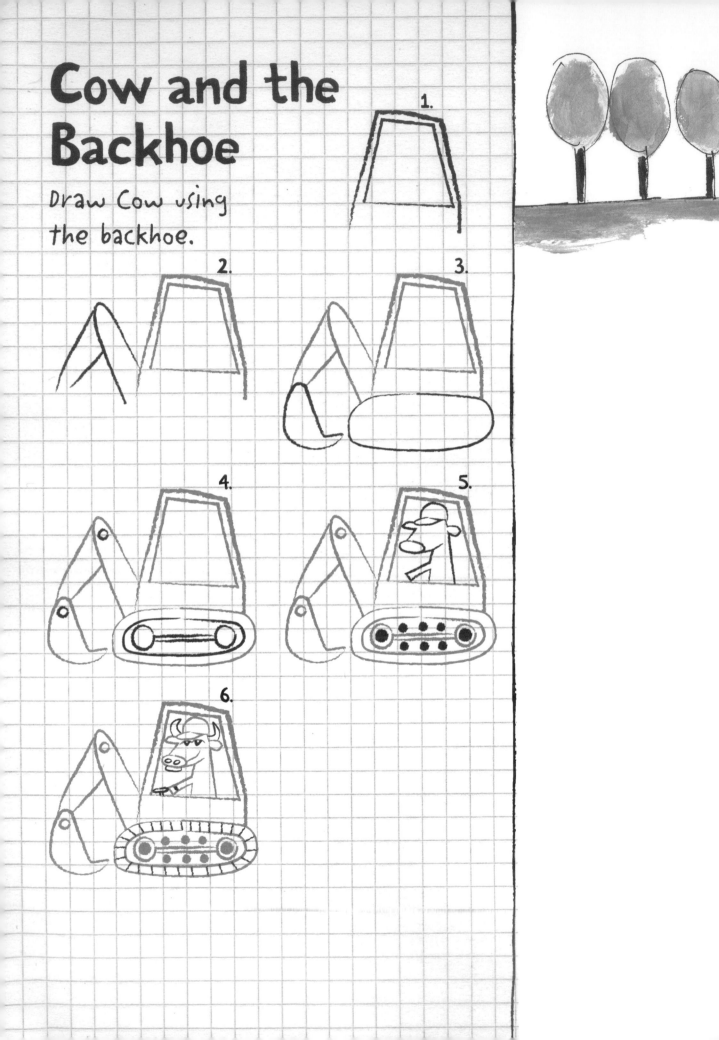

1.

2.

3.

4.

5.

6.

Now try drawing Cow using the backhoe on your own!

Teamwork

Try drawing Pete and his crew putting the finishing touches on the playground!

Pete's New Pet

Draw Pete's new pet goldfish, Goldie.

1.

2.

3.

4.

Now try drawing Goldie on your own!

Fish Food

Draw Pete
feeding Goldie.

Now try drawing Pete feeding Goldie on your own!

Pete the Artist

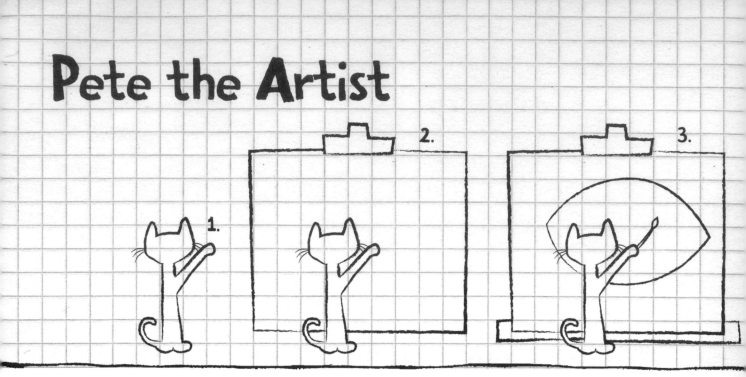

Draw Pete painting a picture of Goldie.

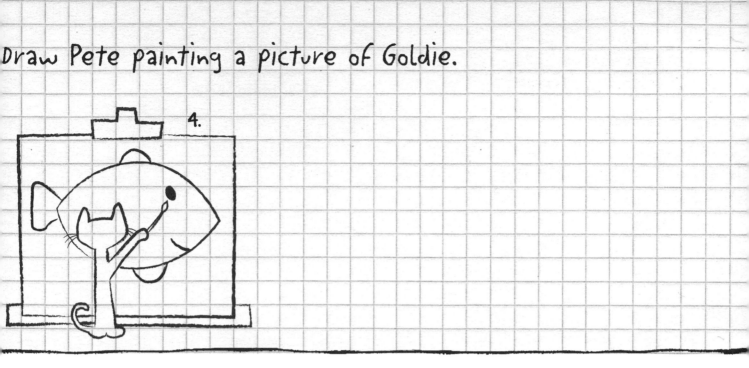

4.

Now try drawing Pete and his painting on your own!

RED

GREEN

BLUE

YELLOW

Gotta Wear Shades

Draw Pete and his groovy shades.

Now try drawing
Pete wearing shades
on your own!

Toad Hog

Draw Grumpy Toad on his motorcycle.

1.
2.
3.
4.
5.

Now try drawing Grumpy Toad riding his motorcycle on your own!

6.

7.

Pete's Pirate Pumpkin

1.

2.

3.

Now try drawing the pirate pumpkin with Pete on your own!

Draw Pete's pirate pumpkin!

4.

Pete's Franken-pumpkin

1.

2.

3.

Now try drawing the franken-pumpkin with Pete on your own!

Draw Pete's franken-pumpkin!

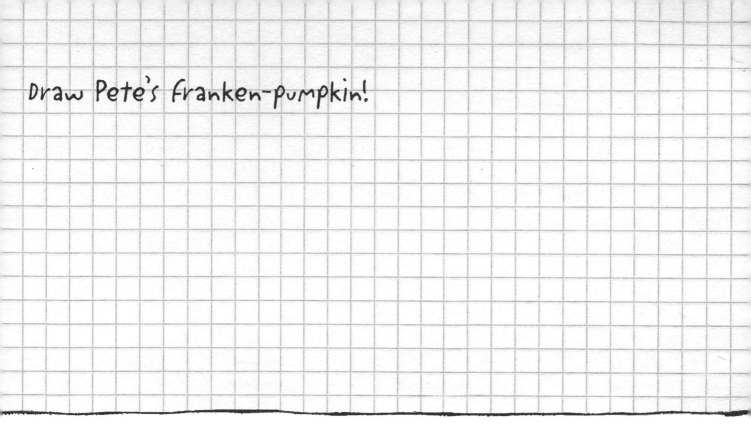

Pete's Vampire Pumpkin

1.

2.

3.

4.

Now try drawing the vampire pumpkin with Pete on your own!

Draw Pete's vampire pumpkin!

Pumpkin Parade

Pete's taking his pumpkins on the road.
Draw the pumpkin skateboard parade!

Family Feast

Draw Pete's big feast.

Now try drawing the feast on your own!

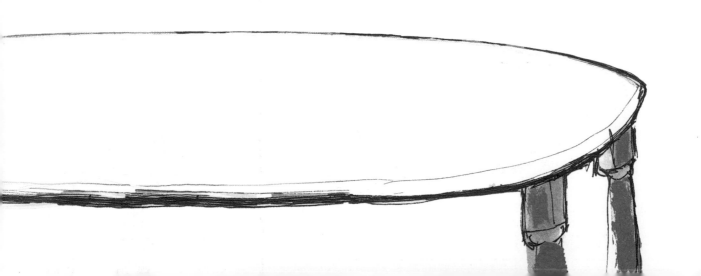

Family Table

Pete, Bob, Mom, and Dad are ready to dig in.

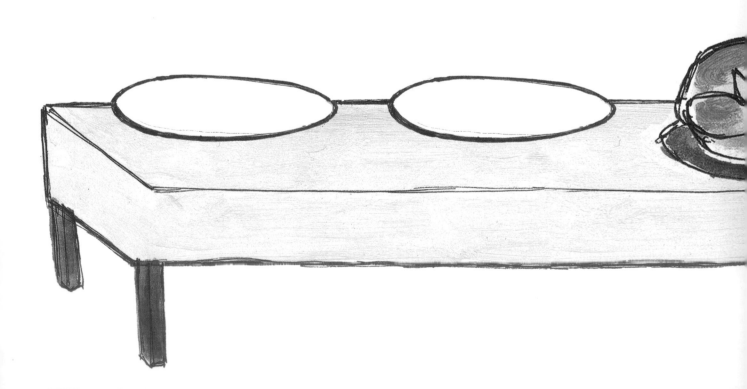

Draw them and their tasty food!

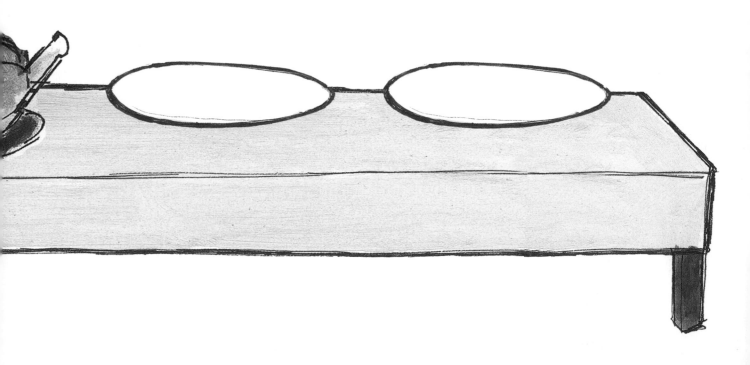

Yard Work

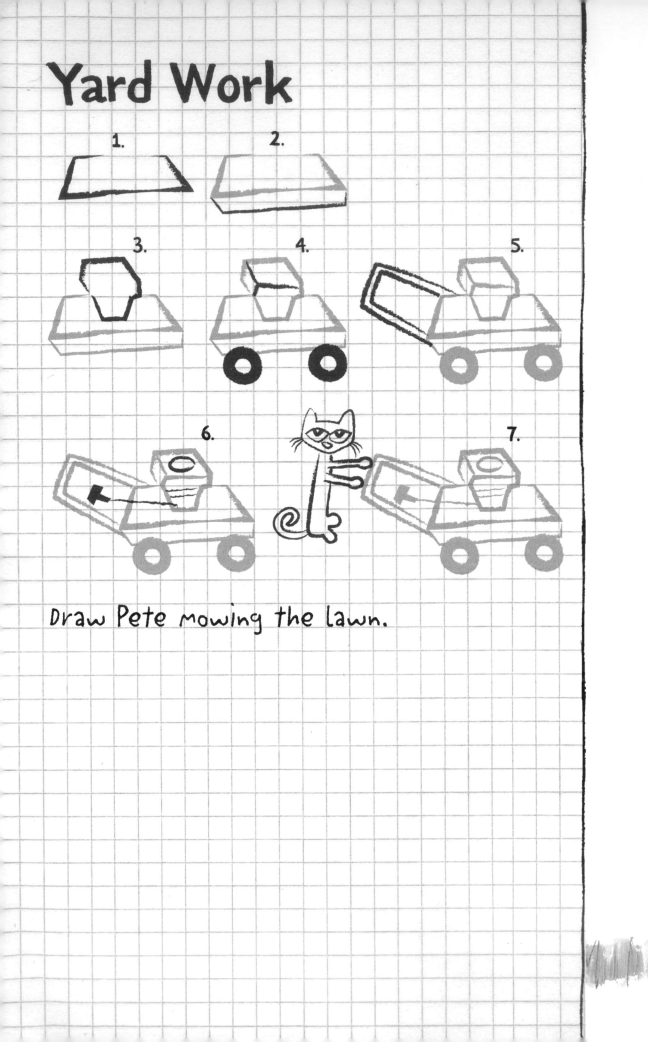

1.
2.
3.
4.
5.
6.
7.

Draw Pete mowing the lawn.

Now try drawing Pete mowing the lawn on your own!

School Safety

Now try drawing Mrs. Gold on your own!

Draw Mrs. Gold, the crossing guard.

6.

All Buttoned Up

Draw Pete wearing his favorite shirt.

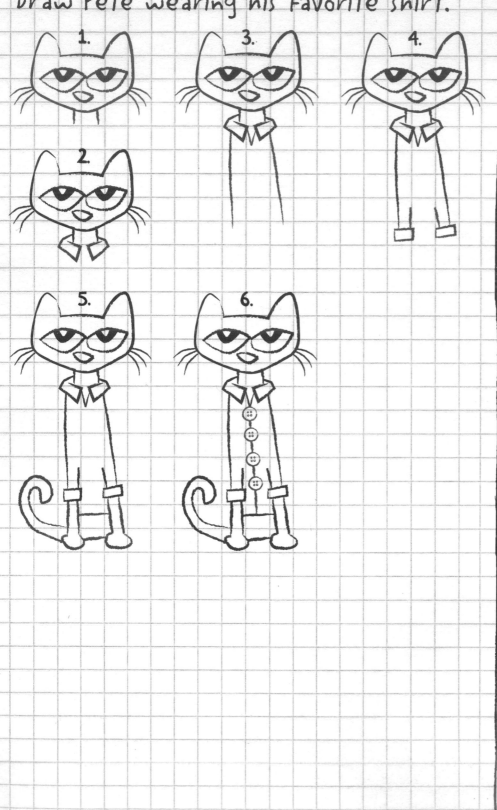

Now try drawing Pete in his new shirt on your own!

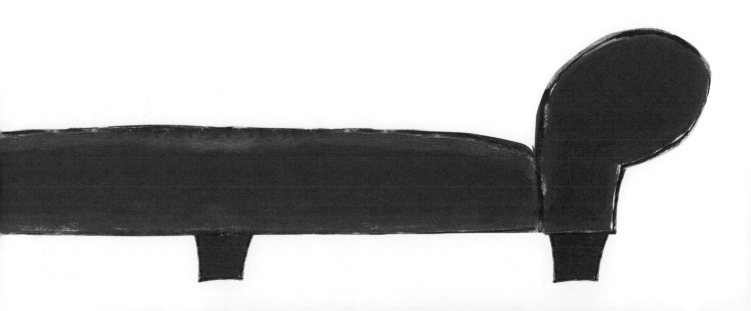

Fleet-Footed Pete

Draw Pete running in a race.

Now try drawing Pete running the race on your own!

Super-Duper Scooper

2. WHIPPED CREAM

1.

1.

2.

1.

1.

2.

1.

ICE CREAM

2.

Draw all the things Pete needs to make an ice-cream sundae.

CHOCOLATE SYRUP

NUTS

Now try drawing Pete making the treat on your own!

Sweet Treat

Pete shares his sundae with Callie.
Draw them enjoying it together!

Sleepy-Time Toad

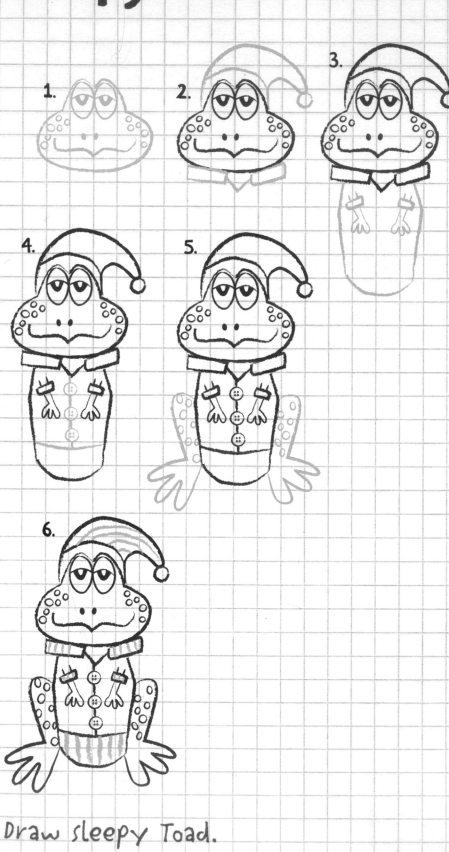

1.
2.
3.
4.
5.
6.

Draw sleepy Toad.

Now try drawing sleepy Toad on your own!

The Cat's Pajamas

Draw Pete all ready for bed.

Now try drawing Pete on your own!

Good Night, Pete!

Pete is getting sleepy. Draw him tucked in bed.

Pete